BLACK HAIR
IN THE 21ST CENTURY
POETRY
That Gets to the Root of the Matter

By
R. J. Rahman

BLACK HAIR

IN THE 21ST CENTURY

POETRY

That Gets to the Root of the Matter

By
R. J. Rahman

Trafford Publishing
1663 Liberty Drive
Suite 200
Bloomington, IN 47403

Trafford Publishing
1663 Liberty Drive
Suite 200
Bloomington, IN 47403
www.trafford.com

Book Cover Design: R. J. Rahman
Graphics for Book Cover and Book layout: Nate Dyer
Photography: R. J. Rahman, Kandyss Watson
Editor: Bobbie Christmas

Library of Congress Cataloging-in-Publication Data
Rahman, R. J.
Black Hair In The 21st Century
Poetry
That Gets To The Root Of The Matter

R.J. Rahman—First Edition

Order this book online at www.trafford.com
or email orders@trafford.com
Most Trafford titles are also available at major online book retailers.
Printed in Victoria, BC, Canada.

ISBN: 978-1-4269-3402-5 (sc)

Library of Congress Control Number: 2010909925

Our mission is to efficiently provide the world's finest, most comprehensive
book publishing service, enabling every author to experience
success. To find out how to publish your book, your way, and have
it available worldwide, visit us online at www.trafford.com
Trafford rev. 5/13/2010

Trafford
PUBLISHING® www.trafford.com
North America & international
toll-free: 1 888 232 4444 (USA & Canada)
phone: 250 383 6864 ♦ fax: 812 355 4082

TABLE OF CONTENTS

Acknowledgments...VII
Introduction IX
Black Hair in the 21st Century - Opening Poem XIII
Photos XIV

MY HAIR KEEPS GOING BACK TO AFRICA (1)

My Hair Keeps Going Back to Africa 17
Hair is Alive 18
Plait-itude 19
Patience 20
Hair Engineering...21

HAIRSTYLING DECISIONS (2)

Black Hair Styling Decisions... 24-25
Relaxed 26
Go Natural 27
Hairstyles 28

IS THAT YOUR REAL HAIR (3)

Is That Your Real Hair? 31
Keep It That Way 32
Brutally Honest...33
Deprogramming Hair Thoughts 34
Fake Has Become the New Real 35-36
The Weave 37
Tracks 38-39
Passing Down Hair Phobias, Half-truths and Problems 40-41

BLACK HAIR POLITICS (4)

It's All in the Hair..44
Uprooted...45
Good Hair-Bad Hair...46
Afros Come To Mind 47
Afro Powerful 48
Hair Wars Introduction 49
Hair Wars.. 50-51
The Definition of Good Hair Introduction 52
The Definition of Good Hair 53-54

HAIR GETS MULTICULTURAL (5)

Hairstyles Reflect Multicultural Modes of Expression 57-58
The European Standard of Beauty is No Longer the Only Standard........59
Were No Longer the Poster Girls for the Weave 60
When Getting it Straight be Black About it..................................... 61-62

THE DON IMUS CONTROVERSY (6)

The Don Imus Incident Introduction 65
The Don Imus Incident Part I 66
The Don Imus Incident Part II..67-69
Ancestral Hairstyles 70

THE FLIP-SIDE OF BLACK HAIR (7)

The Flip-Side of Black Hair Introduction 73
The Flip-Side of Black Hair...74
The Suppression of Black Hair by Black Women Young and Old.............75
The Difference Between Extensions and Weaves 76

BLACK HAIR HAIKUS (8)

Hair Haiku #1...79
Hair Haiku #2...80
Hair Haiku #3...81
Hair Haiku #4...82

AFROS TO BLONDES (9)

Afros to Blondes Introduction 85
Afros to Blondes...86
Someone Else's Kind of Beauty...87
Blond Hair Makes an Appearance 88
The Phrase Blonds Having More Fun Wasn't Meant for Everyone 89
Chocolate Brown Woman with Bleached-Blond Hair...............................90
Brain Storming 91
Mocha, Toffee, Caramel and Cashew Colored Women with Blond Hair...92
Has Progress Been Made? 93

AFTERTHOUGHTS (10)

Shaved Heads 96
Ashamed...97
Unusual...98
Curly Hair..99
Old School Preservation...100
I Perm 101
I Braid 102
Work With What Cha Got 103
Superficial Lessons...104
Let That Stuff Go 105
Backsliding 106
Black Hair Abstract-Women 107
Black Hair Abstract-Men 108
Afro's To 109
Getting To the Root of the Matter 110

OUR WAY OF BEING

Our Way of Being - Closing Poem..113
Bibliography..115
Photo Participants with Businesses 117

ACKNOWLEDGEMENTS

I want to thank my parents; my mother, Khaliqah, who fostered my love for learning and the fine arts in all of its forms and my father, Rafael, who, fostered my love for education and historical research. I would like to thank Dr. Larry Estrada for exposing me to the richness of ethnic cultural studies; Dr. Cornel West and professor/poet Nikki Giovanni for their kind words of encouragement; Reverend Al Sharpton for his courage in confronting major civil rights issues, and holding Don Imus accountable for his derogatory comments; fine artist Anthony Liggins for marketing and promotion; poet Pamela Diana for reminding me of the importance of writing about black men's views concerning black women and hair; Sandra, Poole Editor and Chief of E.K.G literary magazine, thanks for help with editing and giving me insight into how the Afro was viewed during the Black Power Movement of the 1970's; Sabrina for her information concerning disease, hair loss, and its psychological effects; Kandyss for her help with photography; professor/poet Sharan Strange for her help with editing and for suggesting a bibliography be added at the end of the book; Nate Dyer for his words of motivation and graphic design expertise; my brother Abdul for reminding me to write about black women and hair color; my cousin Darlene and her business partner Kimmie for their kindness and hospitality.

I want to thank the brothas for their interest: The ones who asked honest questions while I was writing in my journal at Piedmont Park in Atlanta, Georgia; Pioneer Square in Seattle, Washington; Grant Park in Chicago, Illinois and Central Park in New York City. I also want to thank the brothas that I met on the commuter trains in the US cities listed above. In addition I want to thank the black male forklift drivers, production workers, chemists, medical doctors, engineers, computer scientist, and graphic artists for all of their honest, heartfelt questions concerning black women and hair. When I told the black men I encountered that I was writing a poetry book about black hair, the guys let out a "WOW," followed by a confessional about their experiences with black women and their hair.

I hope that I answered the many questions that I was asked, by black men and women using poetry to explain black hair history in America and the world. Despite the political magnetism that black hair carries, you black men deal and for the most part keep it real. Black women and men are socialized differently when it comes to black hair. Black women react one way while black men react in another. I didn't want you black men to be left out or anything like that so I saved what *I had to say about black men and hair for Chapter Seven, The Flip Side of Black Hair.* I want to thank all of the wonderful men and women who allowed me to photograph them and use their image on the front cover, and a big thanks to the Creator for making all of this possible.

INTRODUCTION

I started writing poetry about hair and other subjects back in 2003. I was motivated to publish the hair poetry that accumulated over the years in journals when viewing the Don Imus talk radio show incident that occurred back in April 2007. This book is for all people who are interested in the subject of black hair and how it is viewed; this book of poetry is also for black women, and men all over the world who are searching for answers concerning the love/hate relationship that they may harbor, to some extent, for their hair. The love/hate relationship towards black hair is a global issue and it is rooted in colonialism and slavery. The negative feelings are passed down from generation to generation; the belief that black hair isn't "good" enough in its natural state. It doesn't matter if you are an African descendent living in the Caribbean, Great Britain, France, United States, Central or South America. It doesn't matter if you're from an African country like Nigeria, Ghana, Kenya or South Africa, no country that has African descendents is immune to the hair dilemma. Why do we think the way we do as black people, about black hair? My wish is to answer the "Why" question and to give a vast history lesson about black hair past and present, using rhythmic poetic verse to evoke understanding and a sincere appreciation for black hair.

BLACK HAIR
IN THE 21ST CENTURY
Opening Poem

BLACK HAIR IN THE 21ST CENTURY

We grew by leaps and bounds in the twentieth century
Our hair went from being pressed to Afros, braids, locks and twists
Before this
It was pressed to fit into mainstream society
It was relaxed to fit into mainstream society
It was straightened to fit into mainstream society
To fit in meant to take away the natural curl from black hair
It's still happening
It's not as bad as it used to be.
During the black power movement in the twentieth century
We went from trying to be other than ourselves
Through our hair
Into
Having pride in ourselves and our hair the way that it is
As it is
Pride in its versatility
We end the twentieth century with a sense of awareness,
Honor, cultural pride and a broadened understanding
Of how far we have come.
We're not out of the wilderness yet.
We still have issues concerning our hair that must not be
Ignored
We must admit that problems exist and do
What it takes no matter how painful to rid ourselves of
The scars left over from colonialism and slavery's past.
When it comes to black hair in the twenty first century
And how it's viewed
It's interconnected to how we view
Ourselves
We still have some work to
Do.

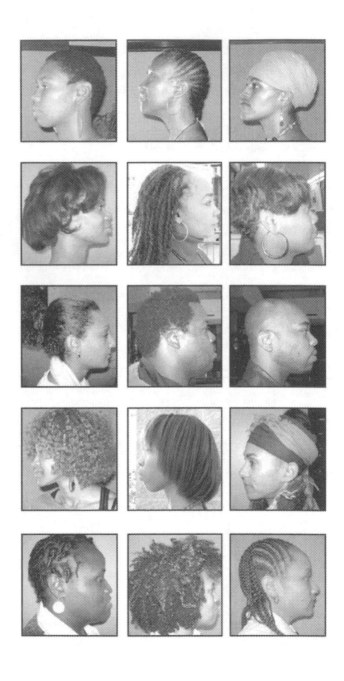

1

MY HAIR KEEPS GOING BACK TO AFRICA

MY HAIR KEEPS GOING BACK TO AFRICA

No matter what I do
My hair keeps going back to Africa.
It reminds me of my ancestors and
The motherland for a millisecond;
It reminds me of my lineage
The generations

That came before me for an instant
Before I start to comb,
When I get caught in the rain,
When I wash it, no matter what I do with it,
Any form of moisture will cause it to curl right back up.

I've tried so many ways to tame it, so to speak
Perming, blow drying, relaxing, hot combing
And flat ironing, temporary forms of straightening
Can't stop your hair from going back,
No matter what you do you will be reminded.
When your new growth grows in after two weeks
Or so you will be reminded;
Low clouds can take you back,
Misty rain can take you back,
Jogging can take you back,
Aerobics can take you back,
Any form of physical exertion
Can take you back;

It's that slight pause that you make when you
See your hair going back to its natural state
It encompasses a psychological change
A slight shift in your thinking;

Like "I said," it happens for a millisecond"
Before you perm, straighten, blow dry
Hot comb, flat iron or relax your hair.

Whether you admit it or not,
That deep breath that you take right before
You begin to comb your hair means
That you are back in Africa.

HAIR IS ALIVE

Hair is alive
It's like plant life or foliage.
Without hesitation it's like vegetation.

Hair is alive
What are you doing with your crop?

Are you adding harmful chemicals that
Will eventually stagnate growth and kill your harvest?
Are you harvesting a bountiful healthy crop?

Are your locks breaking and shedding,
From perming and over processing?

Are you growing your hair with harmful additives?
That can strip it down to the bare phloem core?

Hair is alive
Are you a natural farmer that uses organic compounds?
Is your crop a high maintenance crop with chemicals?
Used at every turn?

Do you prune and cut your hair for maximum even growth?
Or do you allow your foliage to be full of split and un-pruned
Ends with jagged edges,

Hair is alive
It reflects your inner story.

It's a barometer of your thoughts and stress level.
It shows off the ease and disease in your life.

Hair is alive
It's like plant life or foliage,
Without hesitation it's like vegetation.

Hair is alive
"What are you doing," with YOUR crop?

PLAIT-ITUDE

TWISTS——BRAIDS——CURLS——WAVES——LOCKS AND SPIRALS
I'm talking about black hair with
PLAIT-ITUDE
ATTITUDE
LONGITUDE AND LATITUDE
BLACK HAIR
BLACK HAIR
BLACK HAIR
Created with the sun in mind, the moon in mind
And the stars in mind,

The sun is in mind when you see the glimmer of the ringlets
Spirals, curls and coils as they reflect the light from the sun

The moon is in mind when you think about the radiance
The uniqueness of its texture, silky, course and smooth

The stars are in mind when you think about the numerous hairstyles
So much variety along with beads, cowrie shells, and crystals

Metals like copper, silver and gold interlocked within the
Twists, braids, curls and locks to add sparkle and beauty.

Black hair was created to counteract the harsh effects of the suns
Ultraviolet rays, it protects the scalp from the heat

Its beauty, its texture and its strength are incredible feats.

BLACK HAIR IN ITS NATURAL STATE IS THE STRONGEST
HAIR ON THE PLANET

Black hair was created with the sun in mind, the moon in mind
And the stars in mind

IT HAS PLAT-ITUDE, ATTITUDE, LONGITUDE AND LATITUDE.

PATIENCE

HOW CAN BLACK HAIR GROW LONGER?   PATIENCE

HOW CAN BLACK HAIR GROW STRONGER?   PATIENCE

HOW CAN BLACK HAIR BECOME THICKER?   PATIENCE

The main ingredient for black hair MAINTENANCE is
Leaving it alone for a time in a low maintenance style
And having PATIENCE--PATIENCE--PATIENCE

WITH YOURSELF AS WELL AS YOUR HAIR!

BRAIDS teach you PATIENCE
LOCKS teach you PATIENCE
TWISTS teach you PATIENCE

Black hair growth involves an inner growth as well as an
Outer growth and PATIENCE--PATIENCE--PATIENCE

HAIR ENGINEERING

Since the beginning of time when the worship of the goddesses of Africa
was at its prime; ancestors engineered plans in the form of pictorial diagrams.

Fresco Secco designs relics, and symbols left on pyramid walls, to guide us
on how to style our hair;

The first style may have been an Afro or some form of Afro Puff
when you observe the Black Venus misnamed Willendorf.

Prehistoric cave paintings dating back 20,000 years show female
warriors of Africa in flocks with hairstyles engineered in the form of
braids, twists and locks.

Egyptian queens of Africa shaved their heads bald and wore elaborate
beaded wigs with braids and twists; while others braided their
hair into patterned styles that represented the region of their origin

our great ancestral grandmothers left us with markers on how to
style our hair when it's hot or cold when you're feeling shy or bold
hairstyles that look good when you're young or old.

BRAIDS, TWISTS AND LOCKED HAIRSTYLES ARE ENGINEERED FOR US BY US
WITH US IN MIND

THESE HAIRSTYLES HAVE BEEN AROUND SINCE THE BEGINNING OF TIME

2

HAIRSTYLING DECISIONS

BLACK HAIRSTYLING DECISIONS

I have a decision to make and it's about my hair; what to do with it?

I have a decision to make about my hair; how to style it?

I have a decision to make about my hair; whether or not to color it.

I have a decision to make about my hair; should I braid it?

I'M GOING TO PARAPHRASE THIS POEM SO THAT YOU THE READER
CAN MAKE THE CHOICE ON HOW TO FINISH THE REMAINDER OF
THE POETIC VERSE

YOU WILL HAVE TO MAKE A BLACK HAIRSTYLING DECISION

YOUR DECISION WILL REFLECT THE CONDITIONING THAT YOU
RECEIVED IN YOUR ENVIRONMENT WHILE GROWING UP

I'm thinking about twisting, braiding, or locking my hair like a_____

Then again I might straighten my hair in a fashionable way so that
I can have straight hair like a_____

To maintain this westernized hairstyle it would require constant perming
I would have to get touch-ups on my curly hair biweekly or monthly
to have straight hair like a_____

All of this type of reflecting and decision-making is done at a fraction
of a second in periodic increments throughout the days or weeks
before a decision is made about a hairstyle.

Am I going to allow my hair to be curly or am I going to straighten it
and have a westernized look like a_____

Will I take an ancestral stand and override society's imagery program
and braid, twist or lock it like a_____

THIS TYPE OF THOUGHT PROCESS IS DONE IN A FRACTION OF A SECOND
IN INCREMENTS THROUGHOUT THE DAYS AND WEEKS
BEFORE A HAIRSTYLING DECISION IS MADE.

DECISIONS--DECISIONS--DECISIONS

Will I allow the psychological, intrusions concerning another culture's
Standards of beauty prevail?

DECISIONS--DECISIONS

This is the thought process that many women of African descent
go through before choosing a hairstyle.

DECISIONS--DECISIONS

BLACK HAIRSTYLING DECISIONS

RELAXED

When you chemically straighten and relax your hair
The way that you do
Who are you trying to be LIKE?
What are you trying to look LIKE?

And when you are finished chemically relaxing your hair
ARE YOU RELAXED?

When you hot comb or blow dry your hair by any means
Do the ends justify the MEANS?
Who are you trying to be LIKE?
What are you trying to look LIKE?

And when you are finished DO YOU FEEL RELAXED?
Who are you trying to emulate?
Is your hair better when it's straight?
Are you willing to debate?
And if and when you do
Afterwards WILL YOU FEEL RELAXED?

IS STRAIGHT HAIR SUPERIOR? IS CURLY HAIR INFERIOR?
IS THIS TYPE OF THINKING NECESSARY?
IS IT A STATE OF MIND PASSED ON THROUGH GENETICS?
IS IT ENVIRONMENTAL OR JUST PROGRAMMING?

I'm trying to be gentle; talking about this issue can hurt a little.
Have you ever asked yourself these questions?
When I straighten my hair who am I TRYING TO BE LIKE?
What am I trying to look like?
ARE THESE MY NATURAL THOUGHTS?
OR ARE THESE THOUGHTS FROM PAST PROGRAMMING?
PASSED DOWN FROM GENERATION TO GENERATION
From Ancestral Repositioning
This subconscious melodrama being played out over and over
Again without question; to question would make you STOP and think.

WHEN YOU STRAIGHTEN YOUR HAIR THE WAY THAT YOU DO
WHO ARE YOU TRYING TO BE LIKE?
AND AFTERWARDS ARE YOU AT EASE?
ARE YOU RELAXED?

GO NATURAL

I got tired of the constant worry about my hair.
The straightening, curling......
The smell of oil and hair
Burning
I WENT NATURAL

It was liberating; the programming of my thoughts
That straight hair was better than curly hair
Lasted for a moment and then ceased.
Respect for my hair in its natural state
Increased
I WENT NATURAL

I saw my hair grow strong, healthy curly and resilient.
My hair has become an awesome sight to see.
It coordinates itself with my personality.
It amplifies grace, style, and integrity.
I WENT NATURAL

Look at your hair closely now.
Observe the spring,
The curl and the wave
It can teach you things about yourself.
Do it for your spiritual health.
GO NATURAL

Free yourself as well as your hair
You'll soon have more time to spare.
Be amazed by what your hair can do:
For you
To you;
Be you,
GO NATURAL

Your hair can give you peace of mind.
Just listen to what your hair
Is trying to tell you
Stop ignoring it,
Denying its voice
You do have a choice;
GO NATURAL

HAIRSTYLES

HAIRSTYLES can be a way of making a statement.

HAIRSTYLES can be a way of showing off your cultural pride.

HAIRSTYLES can reflect what type of class you're in.

HAIRSTYLES can show off your style, sense, and cultivation.

HOW YOU WEAR YOUR HAIR CAN SHOW YOUR RELIGIOUS
AFFILIATION

HAIRSTYLES can be an outward sign of how much we love ourselves.

How much we hate ourselves.

How much we're trying to be other than ourselves.

HAIRSTYLES can be public, private, political and personal,

They reflect the way we live, how we think; our values

HAIRSTYLES

3

IS THAT YOUR
REAL HAIR?

IS THAT YOUR REAL HAIR?

IS THAT YOUR REAL HAIR? IS THAT YOUR REAL…?

This is the question that I've been asked as a black woman by
black men and women.
My reply in a gentle way is "Yes", this is my hair and lots of
black women have long hair
Believe it or not;
Hair grows from the top of our heads. It's part of our crown and glory.
It's the type of spirit we possess that gives rise to success, pain or glory.
WHY BLACK PEOPLE ARE HAIR CRAZY IS ANOTHER STORY

While our ancestors were enslaved, the European standard of beauty
Was all the rage
Black beauty was vilified, ostracized, disliked and looked upon as savage.
Black curly hair in any form was looked upon as dreaded and awful
for 400 years DURING CHATTEL SLAVERY

Out of that the term dreadlock emerged along with other derogatory terms
TO DESCRIBE BLACK HAIR

THE TERM DREADLOCK IS STILL USED TODAY BUT IN A POSITIVE FORM

The future is now. Black hair styles are becoming respected.
The old programming
From slavery and colonialisms questionable past is slowly being rejected.
Brothers and sisters are beginning to deal and have come into the real.
Real understanding about being who we are as a people and respecting
Our hair as it is whatever the hair texture or type.

WAVES--KINKS--BRAIDS--TWISTS--KNOTS AND LOCKS ARE ALL RIGHT!
IS THAT YOUR REAL HAIR? IS THAT YOUR REAL…?

This is the question that I have been asked as a black woman by
black men and women.
It's time for us to wake-up and look beyond superficial matters.

THERE ARE THINGS IN THIS WORLD THAT ARE MUCH MORE IMPORTANT
THAN THE LENGTH, TEXTURE, AND GRADE OF YOUR HAIR

BELIEVE IT OR NOT!

KEEP IT THAT WAY

I've been told that I looked much better
When I straightened my hair and put it in a ponytail.

I've been told to keep it that way but in a nice way.

I've been told that my hair is beautiful and asked
Why did I have it twisted or braided?
I've been told not to braid my hair by others so
That it can be long and flowing;

I've been told to keep it that way but in a nice way.

After straightening my hair I've been told
Now that my hairstyle is mainstream, I should be
Able to get a man quicker with my long hair in view

I've been told to keep it that way but in a nice way.

Leave it in a nice mainstream hairdo
Whatever you do, just keep it
That way but in a nice way

Certain black people have told me that I have
Good hair and that I do not need to
BRAID, TWIST OR LOCK it up.

BRUTALLY HONEST

Who are you doing it for?
I'M JUST BEING BRUTALLY HONEST
When it comes to your hair who are you relaxing it for?
When you straighten it by any means necessary?
Who are you doing it for?

Are you doing it for yourself and others or is it programming
left over from slavery's past?
When you get caught out in the rain on a foggy spring day
and the first thing that you think about when you arrive
home is grabbing a hair dryer and straightening
your chemically relaxed hair to prevent
It from going back to its natural state?
Who are you doing it for?
I'M JUST BEING BRUTALLY HONEST

IS IT PROGRAMMING LEFT OVER SUBCONSCIOUSLY
IN THE BACK OF YOUR MIND
That your hair isn't good enough the way that it is naturally?
For our distant elders our type of hair was just fine.

AFRICIAN SOCIETIES HAD HAIR CULTURES ESTABLISHED
Hairstyles that reflected status, age, and class
Hairstyles that reflected the nome, tribe or state
Black hair was wonderful without debate

Colonialism CHANGED THINGS
Chattel slavery CHANGED THINGS

THE REMNANT REMAINS WITHIN THE SUBCONSCIOUS
So when you style your hair
Flip and feather your hair
Who are you doing it for?

I'M JUST BEING BRUTALLY HONEST, THINK ABOUT IT.

ARE YOU DOING IT FOR YOURSELF AND OTHERS?
OR
IS IT PROGRAMMING LEFT OVER FROM SLAVERY'S PAST?

DEPROGRAMMING HAIR THOUGHTS

CAN-HAIR GIVE YOU MATURITY?
CAN-HAIR MAKE YOU FEARLESS?
CAN-HAIR STOP YOU FROM BEING ROBBED?
CAN-HAIR

CAN-HAIR GET YOU AN EDUCATION?
CAN-HAIR HELP YOU TRAIN IN A VOCATION?
CAN-HAIR HELP YOU ACHIEVE AND GIVE YOU MOTIVATION?
CAN-HAIR

CAN HAIR STOP YOU FROM GOING CRAZY?
CAN-HAIR PREVENT YOU FROM BECOMING SHIFTLESS AND LAZY?
CAN-HAIR GIVE YOU 20/20 VISION?
CAN-HAIR DIRECT YOU TOWARDS YOUR EARTHLY MISSON?
CAN-HAIR

CAN-HAIR HELP YOU EAT RIGHT?
CAN-HAIR HELP YOU GET IN SHAPE?
CAN-HAIR HELP YOU LOSE WEIGHT?
CAN-HAIR

CAN-HAIR HELP YOU OBTAIN A MASTERS DEGREE?
CAN-HAIR HELP YOU LOCATE YOUR TRUE IDENITY?
CAN-HAIR HELP YOU GET TO WORK ON TIME?
CAN-HAIR

CAN-HAIR MAKE YOU A SUPERHERO?
CAN-HAIR MAKE YOU A STAR?
CAN-HAIR MAKE YOU A SPIRITUALY BALANCED PERSON?
CAN-HAIR

CAN-HAIR HELP YOU EARN A MILLION DOLLARS?
CAN-HAIR HOLD YOUR FAMILY TOGETHER?
CAN-HAIR GIVE YOU COMMON SENSE?
CAN-HAIR
Hair is just that, Hair. It grows on top of your head to protect it from the
Sun's rays; it insulates your scalp on those cold winter days.
Hair can show off your vitality and strength, it depends upon your genetics
If and when it grays; hair is part of your crown, don't let it get you down.
The length, texture and color of it doesn't make the person
Your intentions, deeds and how you carry yourself among other things
DETERMINES WHO YOU ARE REALLY!
HAIR CANNOT AND WILL NEVER HAVE THAT SORT OF POWER
HAIR IS JUST THAT--HAIR!

FAKE HAS BECOME THE NEW REAL

Fake in many cases has become the new real
What you have been given, if it doesn't fit
Society's standards, is looked down upon.

What you have been physically born with in many cases
If it doesn't fit society's standards, it's viewed as
Not good enough

The media says this twenty four hours a day seven days a week.
Just turn on the TV, read a magazine or listen to the radio.
What you're genetically given at birth isn't good enough
It is quietly programmed within your psyche
You're at a loss.

If your hair is not naturally blond you are at a loss.
If your hair isn't long you are at a loss.
If you're not light skinned you are at a loss.
If your butt isn't big enough you are at a loss.
If you're twenty or more pounds overweight you are at a loss.
If your hair is excessively curly you are at a loss.
If your breasts aren't full enough you are at a loss.
If your hair is full of gray you're at a loss.
If you're considered old you're at a loss.

The media says this twenty four hours a day seven days a week.

Don't worry there can be changes made but at a cost.
There can be changes made and it will cost you.

Don't get me wrong some changes are beneficial
But many are cosmetic and are for ego's sake.

Fake is the new real
Fake breasts even if they don't look real are o.k. for some
Why not?
Fake is the new real
Fake hair color may not fit the hue of your skin tone
It may even defy common sense
Why not?
Fake is the new real

Fake eyelashes
Fake lips
Fake nails on your fingertips
Why not?

Fake is the new real.

People are risking their lives for the new real.
People are dying for the new real.
People are worshipping the new real.

People are putting their lives in jeopardy for a quick fix
To obtain the new real

Females are dying from tummy tuck infections.
Females are dying from breast augmentations gone bad.
Females are dying from the toxic side effects of the
Removal of cellulite
What a plight!

Paying money for quick fixes will cost you.

Whatever happened to patience and perseverance?
Exercise
Eating right
And
Self love

Has self love been replaced by physical love?
Has spiritual love been replaced by VANITY?
If so it's a calamity
OR maybe a fad;
In which the female consumer is being had.
It's unreal
Fake
Seems to have become the new REAL

THE WEAVE

BEFORE THE WEAVE

Black women had to work with the hair that they had.

BEFORE THE WEAVE

If your hair looked nice you were given a compliment
and that was that.

BEFORE THE WEAVE

The long hair fantasy was limited to a wig or some form
of clip-on hair attachment and after you took it off
the fantasy was over.

WITH THE ONSET OF THE WEAVE

Now any black woman can have long hair,
if they have the money to pay for it.

WITH THE ONSET OF THE WEAVE

You no longer have to style or comb the hair that you have.

WITH THE ONSET OF THE WEAVE

If you're a black woman and your hair looks nice and it's long,
compliments are frequently followed by
"is that your real hair," type of questions?

THE ONSET OF THE WEAVE

Has some black women questioning themselves as to whether
or not their beauty is even valid without having long straight hair.

THE WEAVE

TRACKS

Tracks
Tracks of hair
Tracks of human hair
Tracks of synthetic hair that give off
The appearance of
Straight hair
Fashionable hair
Acceptable hair
Hair that has been advertised
Hair that has been marketed
Hair that has been approved of
By the media

For Westernized fashion forward hairstyles.
Tracks
Synthetic hair or human hair
Somebody else's hair other than your own
Interwoven onto fabric strips that hold
Synthetic or human hair strands in place.

Tracks
Are used
Within a hairstyling process known as the weave
The weaving process involves

Tracks

Numerous tracks are involved, these

Tracks
Are stretched on top of braids
Then sewn on top of braids
To form a hairstyle that has
A fashionable look
An acceptable look
Just like the hairstyles in the magazines.

Tracks of hair
Tracks of human hair are preferred
Human hair
From India, Korea, Japan, Europe, and South America
Human hair collected to be made part of

38

Tracks

Human hair collected to be crimped
Curled, straightened and feathered
For fashion forward hairstyles.

Braids
Braided cornrows in a horizontal, vertical or circular
Position
Braids are the foundation
Braids are hidden under tracks
Braids are disguised by tracks to look like straight hair.
Braids under tracks are disguised to look like
Fashionable hair
Acceptable hair

Braided hairstyles that are underneath tracks
Are ancient hairstyles
Hairstyles that are thousands of years old
These hairstyles have deep meaning.
These hairstyles are covered by

Tracks

And made to look like straight hair
Acceptable hair
Fashion forward hair
Hair that's advertised
Hair that's marketed

Twenty four hours a day, seven days a week, 365 days a year
To be the type of hair that
You as African descendants
You as African American females
Need to have

Why does your unique form of hair have to be hidden under tracks?

Why does your unique form of hair have to be hidden under a weave?

Why isn't your hair the way that it is
Good enough?

PASSING DOWN HAIR PHOBIAS,
HALF TRUTHS, AND PROBLEMS

We as black women need to stop passing down *Hair Phobias*
Half truths and problems to our daughters,

We need to stop passing down *Hair Phobias* half truths
And problems to our sons,

We need to stop passing down *Hair Phobias* half truths
And problems to the next generation,

We need to think before we speak.
Our way has been accepted by others outside of our culture.
We need to accept our way of:
Braiding
Grooming
Twisting
Locking
Our way of styling is respected

Yet some of us are still holding onto baggage.

Lies told about our hair left over from Slavery's past.

Straight hair isn't better than curly hair.
Whatever type of hair that you were born with is alright
And if you decide to straighten your hair it doesn't make you
Better than a person who allows theirs to be in its NATURAL STATE

Having long hair doesn't make you better than a person who
Has short hair.

You were not born with this type of behavior; this type of thinking
Is learned then it's passed down.

We need to stop it!
Stop passing down
Hair Phobias, half truths, and problems to our daughters, sons,
And the next generation,

They're other forms of beauty besides the Westernized standard
That are just as valid,

Babies are born innocent.   They come straight from God.
They come straight from truth in its purest form.
They come straight from love in its purest form.

They know nothing about hate.
They have to be taught about *Hair Phobias*, half truths and problems.
They don't come here with that type of baggage, it has to be taught.

For thousands of years our hair was just fine the way that it was.
For 400 years our hair was vilified and looked upon as
Primitive and inferior
By others
Within early America
Who couldn't appreciate our physical differences?

Times have changed. Our differences and our beauty
Are now being respected and admired
So it's now time to put a stop to passing down

Hair Phobias, half truths, and problems
To
Our daughters, sons, and the next generation

Let's start passing down
Confidence
Self love
Cultural pride
And
Peace of mind.

4

BLACK HAIR POLITICS

IT'S ALL IN THE HAIR

The lineage of Africa and its offspring's battles with racism,
Discrimination and colonialism

IT'S PRESERVED IN THE HAIR

The African American's sojourn in America
IS REFLECTED IN THE HAIR

How we as descendants of the motherland had to
adapt and survive

IT'S ALL IN THE HAIR

CONSCIOUSNESS--FLEXIBILITY--INVINCIBILITY

IT'S ALL IN THE HAIR

How you look at life
How you look at yourself
How you culturally see yourself
IT'S ALL IN THE HAIR

OUR HAIRSTYLES REFLECT
Adaptation--Relocation--Assimilation--Integration
Isolation--Oppression--Hesitation--Imagination
Separation--Reunification--Self-Revelation--Realization

IT'S ALL IN THE HAIR--IT'S ALL IN THE HAIR
IT'S ALL IN THE HAIR

IT'S ALL IN THE HAIRSTYLE

UPROOTED

UPROOTED
DILUTED
NAPPY ROOTED

UPROOTED

Taken away from the motherland
Taken away from our ancestral family

Diluted, mixing with other races for survival
As a group of people we have experienced:

SLAVERY——CULTURAL INDOCTRINATION——SEGREGATION

And

MIS-EDUCATION
This made some of us hate who we are
This made us hate being NAPPY ROOTED
For being NAPPY ROOTED, STRAIGHT HAIR WAS SUBSTITUTED

Don't blame Madam C.J; she was just trying to make us feel
Better about ourselves

She thought that straightening our hair would help us be respected
NOPE, WE STILL WERE REJECTED

WE AS A PEOPLE HAVE GOT TO COME TO THE CONCLUSION THAT

WE AS A PEOPLE CAN'T PLEASE ANYBODY BUT OURSELVES
AND THAT BEING OURSELVES THE WAY THAT WE ARE IS
OK!

Some of us are still a little bit groggy but most of us
Are OK with being

NAPPY ROOTED

Some of us are still groggy still shaking off the
Mis-education
Segregation and indoctrination of being

UPROOTED

GOOD HAIR--BAD HAIR

GOOD HAIR--BAD HAIR--STRAIGHT HAIR--CURLY HAIR
WHOSE HAIR IS BETTER?

LONG HAIR--SHORT HAIR--THIN HAIR--THICK HAIR
WHOSE HAIR IS BETTER?

WHERE DID THESE CONCEPTS COME FROM?
WHY DO WE THINK THIS WAY?

LIGHT SKIN--DARK SKIN--FAIR SKIN
WHOSE SHADE IS BETTER?

WHERE DID THESE CONCEPTS COME FROM?

WHO'S BETTER; WHAT'S BETTER AND WHY?

WHY DO WE THINK THIS WAY?

It comes out in subtle ways, most of the time it comes
Out in a reactionary haze

Where did the concept of the less black the better come from?

Who couldn't handle our differences?
Who couldn't handle our looks?
Who couldn't handle the texture of our hair?
Who couldn't handle us the way that we are?

WHO COULDN'T HANDLE OUR CULTURE?

WHO COULDN'T HANDLE OUR BLACKNESS?

WHO STARTED ALL OF THIS MESS?
THIS IS NOT HOW IT'S SUPPOSED TO BE

AFROS COME TO MIND

When I think of blackness blossoming and maturing
As it has in America despite the obstacles;
I think about the Afro. Afros come to mind.

The Afro connects to blackness coming into its own as
BLACK POWER--BLACK PRIDE--BLACK INTREGITY
The Afro connects us to the feelings of self worth.
It gave us permission to value who we are.
The Afro is a hairstyle that symbolized the rise out of
OPPRESSION

The Afro comes to mind when I think about the young
Angela Davis defying the odds, and standing up for
WHAT'S RIGHT

The Afro comes to mind when I think about the 1968 Olympics
When those two black brothers stood at the award area
With leather gloves on hands and fists held high.
The Afro comes to mind when I think about Panthers.
Black Panthers fighting against racial injustice.
Brothers and sistas working together to better the community

The Afro comes to mind when I think about Maya Angelou's book
"I Know Why the Caged Bird Sings".
The Afro comes to mind when I think about Gil Scott Herons Spoken word.
The Afro comes to mind when I read Nikki Giovanni's revolutionary
POETRY
The Afro comes to mind when I think about Muhammad Ali.
Floating like a butterfly with his punches that stung like a bee
In the boxing ring

THE AFRO COMES TO MIND WHEN I THINK ABOUT BLACK MOVIES LIKE:
CLEOPATRA JONES, COFFY AND THREE THE HARD WAY

THE AFRO IS THE HAIRSTYLE OF LIBERATION

IT BRINGS TO MIND A CELEBRATION OF BLACK POWER
BLACK PRIDE--BLACK DIGNITY--BLACK INTEGRITY

I THINK OF ALL THESE THINGS WHEN
THE AFRO COMES TO MIND

AFRO POWERFUL

When I think of the term Afro,
powerful comes to mind
Afro puff—Afro practical—Afro powerful

Do you know what power feels like?
Just touch the texture of black hair
In its natural state
Do you know what power looks like?
Just view a well shaped Afro
Round and radiant
Like the shape of the sun.

Do you know what power smells like?
Just add a little bit of hair oil to that fro
And after you're through take a deep breath

Afro powerful

During the civil rights movement when perming
And straightening the hair was all the rage a
Movement began that involved loving
Black hair in its natural state.
A hairstyle emerged that showed off black hair
In its natural state. Black hair round all about the head,
Round like the shape of the sun became known as a
Natural or Afro;

The Afro became one of the major symbols of the
Black power movement

Afro powerful
Afro puff
Afro practical

The Afro empowered black people.
It gave us a sense of pride and respect
The Afro symbolized that black people
From the tips of our toes to the top of our heads
Are fine the way that we are, the way that God made us
What a heritage, what a lineage, what a history

Afro puff—Afro practical—Afro powerful

HAIR WARS
INTRODUCTION

I put together the *Hair Wars* terminology to help bring about an understanding of the subject matter. The term *Hair Wars* is used to represent a series of lawsuits filed in the mid 1980s against Fortune 500 companies in the hospitality Industry. Over a thousand black women filed lawsuits due to discrimination based upon braided hairstyles.

HAIR WARS

Twenty-plus years after the *Hair Wars* ethnic hairstyles
Have become respected,

Twenty-plus years after the *Hair Wars* braided hairstyles
Have become more beautiful, more complex,

Twenty-plus years after the *Hair Wars* braided hairstyles
Have become more diversified.
They've gone beyond
French braid
Cornrows
Braided ponytails

Into
Microbraids
Twists
Lace braids
The intricate braiding techniques
Are modern additions to an
Ancient hairstyling craft

Twenty-plus years after the *Hair Wars*

Braided hairstyles have become
Mainstream

Twenty-plus years after the *Hair Wars*

Braided hairstyles aren't so political.
Braided hairstyles show off cultural pride.
Braided hairstyles prove that other forms
Of beauty exist that are just as valid
As the Westernized standard;

Twenty-plus years ago, black women were fired
For having braided hairstyles in the workplace.

Senators, lawyers, and community activists
Stood beside those brave women
And took on various Fortune 500 companies
In the hospitality industry,

And challenged their corporate views
Of how hair should be
Styled in the workplace

After loss of work, after the pain turmoil and hurt
Over a thousand black women won their lawsuits.

They got compensation, and braids were officially accepted
In the workplace as long as they were professional

Other forms of beauty besides the European form
Had been given a chance

It took lawsuits, protest and standing up for what's right.
It took lawsuits, protest along with standing up for the truth.

Sometimes standing up for cultural pride is necessary,
Sometimes standing up for your very own peace of mind,
No matter what the cost is necessary
Sometimes standing up for what you believe in is necessary.

Making the world a better and more understanding place for
Present and future generations is ABSOLUTELY NECESSARY

THE DEFINITION OF GOOD HAIR
INTRODUCTION

Good hair is a phrase used in the black community to describe hair that's easy to comb. It is usually wavy and close to being straight. This type of terminology comes with much baggage and debate. Bad hair is thought of as being hair that is hard to comb. It's strong hair that has a lot of spring like a coil. Bad hair when combed is referred to in slang terms as kinky or nappy. This outlook on black hair is a remnant left over from colonialism and slavery. The definition of what's good hair and what's bad hair changes according to the life experience of each individual.

THE DEFINITION OF GOOD HAIR

Names and events that take place within this poem are fictional

A woman, a black woman this parable could be about
any woman, well Stacey had beautiful long black hair
she had the type of hair, black people called
Good Hair.

It was long wavy and easy to comb.
This lady had a bout with lupis
and the medication caused her hair to fall out.
Her definition of Good Hair is having a strong healthy
head of hair to comb no matter what type of texture;
Another woman that happens to be a black woman
but this type of scenario could represent any number
of women

Ashley used to complain that her hair was too
kinky and thick to comb, after she received a relaxer
the comb would glide through her hair.
Combing her thick long black hair gave her pride

she had a bout with breast cancer and chemotherapy
caused her hair to shed and then fall completely out.
This woman's definition of Good Hair is any hair that
grows strong and healthy, no matter how thick
no matter how tightly coiled,
to this woman having hair
is a blessing.

Still another woman, she too happens to be black
but what happened to this woman could happen
to any woman of color, Tara had
mid-length black hair she was offered
an internship at an oil refinery;
She was a mechanical engineer.

After she obtained the internship
the supervisors that were in charge of showing her
what her assignment would be did not instruct her
on how to carry out her assignment properly.
The stress of putting up with racism,

discrimination and sexism along with being around
certain chemicals caused Tara's hair to fall out
this black female mechanical engineer believes

that America has come a long way
but it still has a long way to go

Tara believes, having hair that can withstand
the stress of everyday life and unfavorable
work environments would be outstanding

These women are confessing about their hair
and what their definitions of Good Hair is
the idea of having hair period.

Having hair that's strong.
Having hair that grows steadily on top of
their heads.

It doesn't matter if it's wavy
short, long or kinky.

They know that to have healthy
hair no matter what type of form is a blessing.

These women after going through the ordeal
of disease thank God for understanding
and thank God for LIFE

5

HAIR GETS MULTICULTURAL

HAIRSTYLES REFLECT MULTCULTURAL
MODES OF EXPRESSION

HAIRSTYLES HAVE BECOME MULTICULTURAL
MULTIFACITED
MULTI-INCLUSIONARY

Hairstyles in today's society have multicultural undertones.
The multicultural way of thinking in most cases has
Overshadowed the politics of black hair to some degree
Hairstyles can be worn to represent style, fashion
Cultural pride

Still within the black community there are some
Extremes but the ends justify the means.

Hairstyles from different cultures can be worn by
Individuals outside of the culture

This is the multicultural aspect

Straight hairstyles within the black community were
A covert rule for acceptance within society at large
An unspoken socio-economic requirement
Thirty to forty years ago straight hair meant privilege and
Refinement

It was a black female rite of passage
To remove the burden of having curly hair

This ideology exists still today in the black community;
To some degree this view is slowly changing.

The pressure of adopting a westernized hairstyle is still
In existence but it is not as bad as it used to be.
Today braids, cornrows and twists are almost as
Fashion forward as straight hair

Black women if they choose to, can express themselves
Culturally through their hair in its natural state or relaxed
State either way has become acceptable due to the
Practice of MULTICULTURALISM

Due to the acceptance of multiculturalism
Ethnic hairstyles have become more respected
And admired

THE MULTICULTURAL ASPECT CAN BE SEEN
WHEN cornrows are worn by white women
WHEN westernized straight hairstyles are worn
by black women

WHEN Afro puffs and Afros are worn by Asian women

THESE EXAMPLES ARE A FEW OUT OF MANY

WHAT WAS ONCE SOCIALLY UNACCEPTABLE
HAS NOW BECOME MAINSTREAM

At the beginning of the twenty first century
It can be seen that hairstyles are becoming

MULTICULTURAL

MULTIFACETED

MULTI-INCLUSIONARY

THE EUROPEAN STANDARD OF BEAUTY
IS NO LONGER THE ONLY STANDARD

The European standard of beauty is no longer
Just the norm

There are other perspectives that are just as relevant

There's an Asian standard
An African standard
A Hispanic standard
There's a Pacific Islander standard
An East Indian standard
There are a whole host of standards
That are just as relevant as the European standard

Hair has been taken out of context
Hair has been used like skin color and ethnicity
To segregate, discriminate, and separate people

The hair standard has changed
The hair standard has gone global
Respect for the differences in hair
Color, Texture and Style
From many different cultures has
Emerged

Hair, no matter what the type, is meant to be admired
Not scorned.

The European standard of beauty is no longer the only
Acceptable standard, there are other forms of beauty
That are just as relevant.

WE'RE NO LONGER THE POSTER GIRLS FOR THE WEAVE

Black women are no longer the poster girls for the weave
We didn't choose to be.
But somehow we seemed to have fallen into it.
When the subject of hair enhancement comes up
black women are used as scapegoats.

Not all black women have short hair or utilize hair enhancements.
In the form of infusing, weaving or extending;
hair enhancements are used by women of all nationalities
when they want to obtain a particular look
Not having a lot of hair doesn't make you less than a woman.
Hair wasn't formulated to be used as a measuring stick.
or a barometer for calculating your femininity
Somehow within this American society it has silently
been used as a form of female validation.
It's just good to know that black women are no longer the poster girls.

White women have been placed
In the center stage of the hair dilemma
There in the tabloids in droves with bad hair
Bad hair weaves and awful hair extensions.
They have been caught and photographed
During their bad hair days

They have been confessing things, like they don't know
What their natural hair color is.

Due to the fact that they have been stripping
Their natural hair color for so long just to be blond

White women are on TV shows criticizing each other on whose
hair is better and whose hair is or isn't real.
It doesn't matter whether they're red headed, blond or brunette
it's happening in the media.

THE SUPERFICIAL VEIL THAT BLINDS OUR MINDS ABOUT HAIR IS COMING
DOWN HAIR IS PART OF YOUR CROWN, IT ENHANCES THE BEAUTY
THAT YOU ALREADY HAVE AND EVERY CULTURE USES SOME FORM
OF HAIR ENHANCEMENT IN THE FORM OF A WIG, WEAVE OR ATTACHMENT
It's time to put a stop to all of this HAIR HYPOCRISY
It's time to put a stop to all this HAIR CONFUSION
BROADEN YOUR CONSTITUTION

WHEN GETTING IT STRAIGHT
BE BLACK ABOUT IT

The IT that I'm talking about is the hair.
Be culturally aware of it.
Don't lose your mind over it
Don't get too caught up in it.
Straight hair has become part of African Americana.
It was used by black people as a way for gaining
Access and acceptability within the hostile
Environment of early twentieth century America

Straightening one's hair is a choice based on
An individual discretion, but please
Don't lose yourself in the process.
Getting your hair relaxed involves a
Decision making process
IT'S A PROCESS
Straightening curly hair can make
It easier to comb
It can give curly hair styling versatility
Depending upon your outlook
BUT LOOK
Whatever you decide to do with your hair
Is your business; it's all about you.
No matter how you slice it.
It's all about your crown.
A part of you that the whole public
Views on a daily basis
So please when you decide to
Flip and feather it
COLOR it and even
When it is straight,
BE BLACK ABOUT IT.

If you are a BLACK WOMAN, it is a known
Fact that you are going to be physically
Black for the rest of your life
It's a GENETIC THING
It's o.k. to embrace it
EMBRACE who you are.
And if you don't know certain aspects
About your cultural self then

EXTRA, EXTRA, get some books, do
Some research and read all about it

YOU DON'T HAVE TO TRADE IN
THE CULTURAL ASPECTS OF
WHO YOU ARE
Within this Western culture
You do have a choice
PLEASE CHOOSE TO

BE BLACK ABOUT IT

6

THE DON IMUS
Controversy

THE DON IMUS INCIDENT
INTRODUCTION

On April 4, 2007 the talk radio show host of MSNBC's Imus in the Mornings, Don Imus made, offensive comments and directed them toward the Rutgers women's basketball team during its quest for the NCAA Women's Basketball championship. The black collegiate female basketball players, along with black women from all walks of life, were directly affected and highly outraged by his statements.

Don Imus was not alone. He and other sports commentators called the young black female basketball players who represented Rutgers University a whole host of degrading names. The comment that struck a nerve and ignited an onslaught of controversy was the phrase Don Imus used, "Nappy-Headed Ho's" it was this horrible comment that made media headlines all over the country and led to the cancellation of his talk radio show along with his immediate firing. He ultimately was hired by another station, but actions were taken that lead to his dismissal at MSNBC. His racist and sexist comments affected the entire black community. Until this type of mindset gets dealt with; the larger issue of the degradation of black women in both hip-hop and mainstream culture, this is in no way finished.

THE DON IMUS INCIDENT PART I

HARSH REALITIES

Don Imus, his comments gave young
blacks of the twenty first century a

Glimpse

Of how their not so distant elders
were viewed in America during the
nineteenth and mid-twentieth century,
he showed us with his usage of the phrase

"Nappy-Headed"…

How black hair was once viewed in early America.
He gave us a glimpse of how black hair was used
to vilify black people for centuries.
Through his satirical comments he gave us a
Demonstration.

He gave us a glimpse into how
black hair and black skin color were used
as tools to humiliate black people and
divide black people for centuries
Through his words, he gave us a
Demonstration.

He reminded us how dark skin and tightly curled
hair mythology meant inferiority.
He reminded us how light skin straight hair
mythology meant superiority and acceptance.
He illustrated this through his words;
through his comments how
The game of race was played
within the American Society.

He gave us a demonstration
He gave us a peek
He gave us a glimpse

Don Imus, his inappropriate comments,
brought up Harsh Realities.

THE IMUS INCIDENT PART II

DON IMUS AND OTHERS SAID MORE THAN JUST
NAPPY HEADED …

Don Imus and a whole host of sports and media commentators
used derogatory statements to describe the Rutgers women's
basketball team.

Don Imus called the young women playing basketball rough girls
he said more than just Nappy-Headed…
Another sports commentator stated that the young women
playing basketball for Rutgers looked like,
Memphis Grizzlies or Toronto Raptors.

Don Imus and others said more than just Nappy-Headed…
One other commentator called the young women playing
basketball, "Hard-Core Ho's "

Don Imus and others said more than just Nappy-Headed…

Don Imus agreed with a sports commentator
who compared the visual of the Rutgers women's basketball team
playing the Tennessee woman's basketball team for the NCAA
Women's Basketball championship to a scene from a Spike Lee movie
called *School Daze* when the Jigaboos competed against the Wannabees,
the Jigaboos symbolized Rutgers, the darker skinned players with dark
jerseys; the Wannabees symbolized Tennessee, the lighter skinned players
with white jerseys.

THIS IS ALL A PART OF PUBILC RECORD

I JUST WANTED TO REMIND EVERYBODY THAT THERE WAS
MORE BEING SAID DURING THE "IMUS IN THE MORNING",
COMMENTARY THAN JUST "NAPPY-HEADED HO'S"
Don Imus and others
called the young collegiate black female basketball players
names that were used during
America's racist and not so distant Jim Crow past.

Don Imus and others called future Black Female:
DOCTORS
LAWYERS

SCIENTISTS
ENGINEERS
ARTISTS
SPORTS STARS
DIPLOMATS
Future mothers and
FEMALE CEO'S

"NAPPY-HEADED HO'S"
Don Imus and others used names that were used by
racist whites to dehumanize and degrade African Americans.
names that were used in some cases up until the
mid-twentieth CENTURY
Names used before and during the civil rights movement.
NAMES USED BEFORE THE YOUNG AFRICAN AMERICAN FEMALE
BASKETBALL PLAYERS WERE EVEN BORN
Their racist statements not only affected
African American women on the collegiate level
their statements affected African American women
from all walks of life.
THEIR RACIST STATEMENTS REFLECT AN OUTRIGHT DISRESPECT
FOR BLACK PEOPLE IN GENERAL
DON IMUS, HIS RACIST STATEMENTS WERE DIRECTED TOWARDS
BLACK WOMEN AND THEIR UNIQUE FORM OF HAIR

Black women:

with Afros
Relaxers
Perms
Weaves
Braids
Twists
And Locks

His statements were directed
towards black women with
hair textures from the
MOTHERLAND
Meaning
AFRICA

WOMEN WITH A SOMEWHAT RECENT AFRICAN LINEAGE
WITH A TIGHTLY CURLED FORM OF HAIR
Were affected
for the most part AMERICA as a whole HAS GROWN
AMERICA as a whole HAS MATURED
The behavior from the talk radio show host Don Imus was not
tolerated, Mega Fortune 500 companies withdrew their
sponsorship
This shows that AMERICA has grown as a country.
and has learned
to respect the racial and cultural differences of others
AMERICA still has a long way to go
but AMERICA has grown.
Don Imus his racist statements were the cause of his
FIRING
His statements were an embarrassment to all AMERICANS
with a conscious

HIS STATEMENTS WERE A LITMUS TEST
For the African American community

HIS STATEMENTS REFLECT the much larger issue of the degradation
and objectification of black women in both hip-hop and mainstream
culture.

HIS STATEMENTS SHOWED how certain forms of hip-hop music
on the radio airwaves is AFFECTING how AFRICAN AMERICAN women
are being viewed across the country and throughout the WORLD

HIS FIRING AND REHIRING

HAVE opened up a
Much needed DIALOGUE
of issues that concern SELF IMAGE;
cultural pride and accountability
WITHIN THE BLACK COMMUNITY

ANCESTRAL HAIRSTYLES

The young African American women on the
Rutgers women's basketball team had
ANCESTRAL HAIRSTYLES
They had hairstyles that were worn
By their ancestors some 4,000 years ago

These young black females while playing for
The NCAA women's basketball championship
Had braids in their hair.

They had braids in one form or another
Hairstyles that were
Engineered by their African ancestors
To withstand the water
To withstand the heat
To withstand the everyday wear and tear of the
EVERYDAY

They wore hairstyles formulated to tame and
Beautify the strongest human hair
On the Planet

These young ladies had hairstyles that
Were worn by great African female:
QUEENS
PHAROHS
CONQUERORS
WARRIORS
And LEADERS

Hairstyles that were created for the
Uniqueness, originality
And beauty
Of black women

7

THE FLIP-SIDE OF BLACK HAIR

THE FLIP-SIDE OF BLACK HAIR
INTRODUCTION

This chapter consists of two essays and a poem. In the essay entitled the Flip-Side of Black Hair the term Flip-Side is used to describe the behavior patterns that certain black men exhibit towards black women's hair and how its styled. The second essay entitled The Suppression of Black Hair by Black Women Young and Old and the poem entitled The Difference between Extensions and Weaves are both self explanatory.

THE FLIP-SIDE OF BLACK HAIR

Some black men say that they admire black women with natural hairstyles. Some say that black hair in its natural state is beautiful, except when they see a group of black women with Afros, locks, twists and braids. When presented with a choice between the women with the weaves and the women with the natural hairstyles most black men choose the weave. Some brothas make choices using the FLIP-SIDE of their psyche and go for what it is they're socially conditioned to accept.

When presented with the choice between curly or straight hair, some brothas say one thing and prefer another straight hair is usually chosen; the philosophy of keeping it real changes when it comes to socialization, acculturation, and indoctrination. The FLIP-SIDE comes through; natural thoughts of how hair should be are replaced by your subliminal education.

Subliminal education is the type of learning that happens when you watch television commercials, read magazine advertisements, or listen to certain types of music on the radio. Its influence is far reaching, and it happens by default seven days a week, 365 days a year.

If you do not receive education about your culture in some form and the media isn't deflected, you will follow what you see to some degree psychologically. Hair in some cases can be used as a barometer of what you are socialized to accept.

Some brothas talk the talk but don't walk the walk and are part of the reason why black women spend excessive amounts of money on their hair. Some black men are part of the motivation that causes black women to risk their hair, hair follicles and scalp to toxic chemicals and glues that in some cases do much more harm in the long run than good.

Some sistas would retain their natural hairstyles and not give into perms, relaxers and weaves if they felt that they had a choice.

Many black women think that in order to compete with women from cultures that have long hair, they have to straighten their hair, sew in excessively long weaves, or become blondes to gain the much needed and valued attention from black males.

THE INFLUENCE BEHIND WESTERNIZED WAYS OF STYLING HAIR HAS CAUSED SOME BLACK MEN TO THINK ONE WAY AND ACT ANOTHER WAY.

THE PRESSURES ASSOCIATED WITH CONFORMING TO WESTERNIZED BEAUTY STANDARDS HAS CAUSED SOME BLACK WOMEN TO THINK ONE WAY AND APPEAR ANOTHER WAY.

IT'S ALL PART OF THE FLIP-SIDE OF WHAT SOME BROTHAS AND SISTAS THINK WHEN IT COMES TO BLACK HAIR.

THE SUPPRESSION OF BLACK HAIR
BY BLACK WOMEN YOUNG AND OLD

It used to be that young black females between the ages of five and twelve would just get a press and curl. This happened in the 1940s, 1950s, 1960s and 1970s. In the 1980s, some mothers began to give their young daughters relaxers to straighten their hair and hair extensions to give length and staying power to braided hairstyles. From the late 1980s, 1990s and on into the new millennium, all three hairstyles are still being used: press and curl, relaxer and braided hair extensions. Now a new form of styling young black female hair has emerged and it's called the weave.

What was once used just by young adult females in the mid 1980s is now being used by young black girls at earlier and earlier ages. Young black girls are being informed through peer pressure and media pressure that their hair the way that it is, in its natural state, isn't good enough. They are being shown in subtle ways that their hair has to be changed; their hair isn't good enough in its natural state and it has to be straightened; their hair isn't good enough in its natural state, so you have to add color to it or add length to it, cover it up or hide it under something that has the appearance of acceptability. That's right, black women young and old are affected with the belief that their natural hair isn't good enough! Most feel that they must do whatever it takes to cover it up or change it.

Young black females nowadays aren't really given a chance to deal with their hair in its natural state; they have a choice, but through socialization from the media, the chance becomes not a chance for some. Hairstyles have become multicultural to some degree, but at what cost? Hairstyles have multicultural overtones mixed with "black hair isn't good enough" undertones.

A segment of young black inner-city female youth are screaming for attention through their hair. Some are dying their hair red, green, orange, purple, and yellow for some form of acknowledgement and recognition. While others have parents that cannot afford the expense of weaves, relaxers or extensions are isolated and left out of the popular crowds; and have to deal with feelings of inadequacy because they have to style their hair in its natural state. A small segment of black women of varying ages are wearing wigs in questionable ways, and weaves styled in unfavorable ways. Some black women are putting hair color in their hair that might be fashion forward by Western society's standards. In reality the color added to their hair doesn't go with the hue of their brown skin. In many cases it seems to be noticeable to viewers within the general public, but ignored by the women with the curious hair color. Black women young, old, and in-between have to fight the conditioning, fight the thought process involved in thinking that their hair isn't good enough. Black women must get beyond the multicultural overtones mixed with "black hair isn't good enough" undertones.

THE DIFFERENCE BETWEEN
EXTENSIONS AND WEAVES

The difference between extensions and weaves
For people who don't know.

The difference between extensions and weaves
Some people think that they are one in the same.

The difference between extensions and weaves
There is a difference
They are both forms of hair enhancement.

Extensions and weaves can involve either natural or synthetic hair.
Extensions involve strips of hair natural or synthetic braided into
A section of a person's natural hair;
This is done to add length to short or medium length hair
Or to add depth and thickness to long hair
Extensions usually involve braided or twisted hair styles.
Extensions also act as a barrier. They can slow up the hair locking
Process and prolong the beauty of braided hairstyles
Weaves
Weaves involve synthetic and human hair interwoven on to
Tracks
These tracks are cut into wide strips and sewn onto
Braids that are tightly braided and interlocked onto the scalp
Tracks are sewn onto a particular form of braid called
The cornbraid
The cornbraid when braided is called a cornrow due to
Its resemblance
To a vertical row of corn on the cob
Weaves are a form of hair enhancement
Used by black women, white women and
Women of different nationalities to
Obtain Westernized hairstyles
Weaves are used for a whole host of
Reasons
But for the most part
They are used to add length
To short or medium length hair
There is a difference;
Weaves and extensions aren't the same both are
Styling techniques involved in the
HAIR ENHANCEMENT PROCESS

76

8

BLACK HAIR HAIKUS

HAIR HAIKU #1

My hair is curly
It's black, curly, and strong
Been that way since birth

HAIR HAIKU #2

It can take you back
When you see your hair revert
Back to Africa

HAIR HAIKU #3

I have pride in it
Pride in African hairstyles
Cornbraids, twists, and locks

HAIR HAIKU #4

It's all in the hair
The difference comes from its shape
Black hair is unique

9

AFROS TO BLONDES

AFROS TO BLONDES
INTRODUCTION

The poetry within this chapter is not out to bash any black women who have naturally light sandy brown or blond like hair. This poetry is meant to jar your mind and make you think about the behavior pattern that may or may not be present when it comes to adding hair color to your hair.

AFROS TO BLONDES

From Afros to Blondes what is going on?
From Afros to Blondes what is going on really?
Are black women seeing things clearly?
Have we thrown in the towel?

The I can't beat it join it mentality has
Become more than just a reality
From Afros to Blondes, what is going on?

Have we given up when it comes to embracing our identity?

Yes some black women have golden brown hair naturally.

Yes some black women have sandy brown hair with blond
Streaks here and there naturally

Their features match their hair type.
The hue of their skin matches their hair type.
These women are few and far between.

In between these women are the majority.
Multitudes of black women with dark brown and black hair
With features to match; what's the catch!
What's going on?

The Black power mindset along with the Afro brought in
The trend of black hair acceptance;

Shattered the glass ceiling of westernized beauty standards,
And established black as beautiful.

The Black power movement opened up the door
For hairstyles with Afro centered flair but some of
Us dare to go blond what's going on!
Having highlights is one thing,
Having red, pink and purple hair is one thing,
HAVING BLACK HAIR WITH FEATURES TO MATCH
AND DECIDING TO GO BLOND IS A WHOLE NOTHER
STORY.

From Afros to Blondes what is going on?

SOMEONE ELSE'S KIND OF BEAUTY

Blond Hair
Blond Hair

It was forced upon a select breed of
black women of a lighter hue during slavery.

These women had to put up with
someone else's KIND of beauty standards as an
Unspoken requirement.

These women had to satisfy the desires of their owners
And the fantasies of the men that they were sold to.

They had to wear blond wigs of the powdered KIND
For survival.

Someone else's KIND of beauty, someone else's outlook
Had to be embraced, had to be utilized.

The outgrowth that came from the mandatory usage of
Someone Else's KIND of beauty

Was a strange KIND of acceptance?
And from that a strange KIND of favoritism emerged;

For the select breed of black women with a lighter hue

This KIND of behavior flourished during slavery.
And after 400 years;

Blond hair became imprinted onto the psyche of
Black Women

Black women that were the descendants
Of African women who were uprooted

And taken away from the motherland
and forced to work in a strange land.

BLOND HAIR MAKES AN APPEARANCE

What was once forced upon a select few during slavery seems to keep
coming up many years after slavery.

This black women and blond hair thing seems to keep popping up.
Just when you think that it's gone
is when it seems to make an appearance.

It shows up through wigs worn by black women in the 1950s

It shows up through bouffant wigs worn by black women in the 1960s

After the civil rights movement and during the
Black power movement of the 1970s blond hair seems to
make an appearance in the form of blond Afros and blond Afro wigs.

It can be seen to a small degree in the 1980s
but in the 1990s and on into the new millennium, blond hair shows up
incorporated in dreadlocks and braids.

What was once forced upon a select breed
of black women of a lighter skin color during slavery,
has crossed over into the desires of black women with darker skin tones
in the late twentieth and early twenty first century.

Sometimes blond hair acceptance by
black women with darker skin tones seems to defy logic
and common sense.

Blond hair on black women with dark skin color—

Is it a passing fad that keeps coming back?

Or is it someone else's version of beauty making
an appearance?

THE PHRASE BLONDES
HAVE MORE FUN WASN'T
MEANT FOR EVERYONE

The phrase blondes have more fun wasn't meant for EVERYONE
And that's okay! it's okay to have phrases that are culturally specific.

IF THE PHRASE BLONDES HAVE MORE FUN
WERE FUNDAMENTALLY TRUE
Then blondes would be the only group of people having fun in a world where
the majority of its inhabitants are people of color with dark pigmented hair.
The majority of the people in the world would have no fun.

THE PHRASE BLONDS HAVE MORE FUN IS CULTURALLY SPECIFIC TO THE
EUROPEAN CULTURE

Even though the western media pushes many phrases about
blondes having fun and being the ultimate standard of how
beauty is measured in the west.

IT ALL FALLS INTO THE CATEGORY OF A EUROPEAN POINT OF VIEW
Many Americans stars with European ancestry take the phrase, blondes have
more fun literally and when most of the dark haired white actors reach star
status they strip the pigment from their hair to become blond. Some stars
keep their new blond locks. While others dye their hair back to its original
color; most movie stars realize that the blond thing isn't what it's
HYPED UP TO BE

THE BLOND THING ISN'T FOR EVERYBODY IN THE EUROPEAN CULTURE
The phrase blondes have more fun may be a confidence building or morale
boosting phrase for a particular subset of Europeans but even still the phrase
wasn't meant for EVERYONE

JUST LIKE THERE IS NO ONE GROUP OF PEOPLE IN THIS WORLD THAT HAVE
THE COMPLETE OWNERSHIP OF BEAUTY

BEAUTY IS INFINITE

Beauty is beyond hair color, skin color and hair length
it's beyond categories.

Oh, and did I mention that the phrase blondes have
more fun WASN'T MEANT FOR EVERYONE

CHOCOLATE BROWN WOMAN
WITH BLEACH-BLOND HAIR

CHOCOLATE BROWN WOMAN WITH BLEACH-BLOND HAIR
What's going on?
Why are you trying so hard to be other than yourself?

Why are you trying so hard to cover up?
The looks that God gave you
The genetics that God gave you
The beauty that God gave you

Covertly vilifying your looks
YOUR culture
YOUR integrity
YOUR identity

TO LOOK LIKE SOMEBODY THAT YOU CAN NEVER TRULY BE
CHOCOLATE BROWN WOMAN WITH BLEACH-BLOND HAIR

YOU'RE A DECENDENT OF AFRICA WHETHER YOU LIKE IT OR NOT
IT'S OBVIOUS

You are a DECENDENT of Africa in America
And yes this makes you an African American
If you choose to accept the title

CHOCOLATE BROWN WOMAN WITH BLEACH-BLOND HAIR
The cat's out of the bag
The rabbit's out of the hat
The chickens have come to roost

The subconscious psychological battle that you're going through
Is no longer a secret; it has manifested itself
THROUGH YOUR HAIRDO

Everybody can see that you're trying really hard to be something
That you weren't created to be

WHY CAN'T YOU SEE?

BRAIN STORMING

Blondes having more fun
Is a culturally specific phrase
Just like
Black is beautiful

Blondes having more fun
Is a culturally specific phase
Just like
Black is beautiful

Blondes having more fun
Is culturally specific

Black is beautiful
Is culturally specific

Blondes having more fun
Is culturally specific

Black is beautiful

Black is beautiful

Black——Is——Beautiful

MOCHA, TOFFEE, CARAMEL AND CASHEW COLORED WOMEN WITH BLOND HAIR

Mocha, toffee, caramel and cashew colored women
I am talking about black women with various shades of
brown

Sporting blond hair, "why", when you are so beautiful?
In your natural state, this is a known fact
THAT HAS BEEN PROVEN WITHOUT DEBATE.

Mocha, toffee, caramel and cashew colored women
Black women with various shades of brown

Why are some of you trying so hard to eliminate
The pigment in your hair; this thing I'm talking about is
BEYOND MERE HIGHLIGHTS AND STREAKS

Mocha, toffee, caramel and cashew colored women
Black women with various shades of brown

Some of you have a blond ambition when it doesn't seem
VISUALLY LOGICAL

Mocha, toffee, caramel and cashew colored women
Black women with various shades of brown

Black women with blond hair, what are you trying to prove?
It seems as though you are fighting some sort of a
UPHILL BATTLE FOR ACCEPTANCE

Mocha, toffee, caramel and cashew colored women
Black women with various shades of brown

Fashion is one thing; fads are another. This blond thing
IS IT STYLE OR IS IT ASSIMILATION?

Mocha, toffee, caramel and cashew colored women
Black women with various shades of brown
What is it going to take?
To make you understand that you are
BEAUTIFUL,
The way that you are
IN YOUR NATURAL STATE

HAS PROGRESS BEEN MADE?

Black hair to blond hair
Locks to blond locks
Braids to blond braids

Has progress been made?

Hair has become an accessory for some
Like jewelry, purses and shoes.

While others feel that they are made better by superficial changes
In hair color, structure and length, with all of these changes
Some of us are at a loss when it comes to questions, concerning identity.

Has progress been made?

This blond thing is it a manifestation of dual consciousness gone wrong?
Why are black women trying to imitate white women with blond hair?
Is it some sort of psychological snare?

Has progress been made?

If we really knew about our culture, if we really embraced our culture
Would blond hair on black women's heads be necessary?

Has progress been made?

Some of us are hiding behind a blond hairdo trying to dodge the real issue.
Some of us are using blond hair as a mask or a shield to hide
personal dilemmas.

Has progress been made?

Or is it a malicious attempt to fit in and be accepted.

Is it a last ditch effort?

Skin color, hair color and hair texture are all interrelated when it
Comes to the subject of black cultural identity

HAS PROGRESS BEEN MADE?

10

AFTERTHOUGHTS

SHAVED HEADS

Black hair, what was once looked upon with pride is now looked
Upon with indifference, and in some cases hate.
How did it happen?

SLAVERY

SLAVERY HAPPENED!

When black men and women were captured during slavery their heads
were shaved and if it did not happen during their capture then it
happened on the slave ships.

Their heads were shaved to remove any form of
cultural connection with Africa

These black men and women were not allowed to have picks
or any form of African traditional grooming aids for their hair.
Black men and women were treated like chattel.
They had to work from sun up to sun down during slavery.
They were not given much time to groom themselves.

Black hair became matted and undesirable.

What was once prized for its beauty and uniqueness had to be covered up?

What was once a vehicle for art and culture had to be hidden!

What was once glorified for power and spiritually had become
something savage and strange;

After the passing of 400 years,

Black hair became an instrument of grief and sorrow for its bearers.
It became an outright embarrassment to have black hair in its natural state.

The Embarrassment
Manifested into a form of SELF HATRED
Along with that came a hatred for black hair

All of this came about through a violation that occurred when heads were

SHAVED

ASHAMED

Some of us treat our hair like it's a disease, burden or problem.
Some of us are ashamed.

The wigs and weaves that we apply to our heads, make some of
Us look like we're going through chemotherapy when we're actually
Physically healthy

Some of us treat our hair like it's a disease, burden or problem.
Some of us are ashamed.

We put our minds through so much stress.
We put our scalps through so much stress.
We put our hair through so much stress.

The stress comes from deep seated feelings of hair inadequacy.
That stems from being ashamed of our unique hair type;
Despite black power the Afro and all of its hype

Some folks still treat their hair like it's a disease, burden or problem.
We need to stop giving into bad habits.
We need to start challenging the way we look at ourselves,

Remove the veil of shame and stop being ashamed.

UNUSUAL

For some black women dealing with their hair in its natural state
Has become unusual,

Combing their hair in its natural state has become unusual.
Viewing their hair in its natural state has become unusual.

The curly stuff that grows out from the scalp is a nuisance.

Wigs have become a preference.
Weaves have become a preference.

Fantasy has become the norm
Reality has become unusual.

Viewing, dealing and functioning with our hair in its natural state
Kinky, curly or straight for some has become

Unusual

CURLY HAIR

Curly hair is wild; straighten it—

It's unruly; tie it up!

It's wild; cover it up!

It's unruly; tame it!

It's wild; change it!

Curly hair represents difference
Curly hair represents ethnicity

OLD SCHOOL PRESERVATION

Can't go swimming

Can't jump rope too fast

Can't run as much

Can't play tag for too long

It could mess up my hair.
It could get me into trouble.
This press-n-curl has to last
at least a week.

I PERM

To release the curl

I perm

To rid my hair of its natural spring

I perm

To feel my hair blowing in the breeze

I perm

To make my hair easier to comb

I perm

To have a fashion forward look

I perm

I BRAID

To bring about a change of pace

I braid

To show off cultural pride

I braid

Because of the convenience

I braid

To be relieved from constant styling, perming
flat ironing, blow drying and hot combing

I braid

To have more time to think

I braid

WORK WITH WHAT CHA GOT

Work with what cha got and make it look good.
Black people have always been resourceful.
This doesn't stop with our hair.
Some of us need to work with
what we have been given.

And stop chasing after what others have.

Let's take the hair that we have and
Embrace it
Respect it.
We have always been able to take
something from nothing and make something
Our hair is that something.

It's unique and full of potential

Let's stop cursing its potential
Let's stop hiding its potential
Let's stop replacing its potential

We have so many beautiful hairstyles
to choose from——

Stop living in fear of your crown and glory.
Work with it.
Work with what cha got.

SUPERFICIAL LESSONS

When history is studied without being registered
Within the consciousness it becomes a superficial lesson.

When culture isn't passed down and understood it can fall
Victim to becoming a superficial lesson

Some black people think that having an Afro, braids or locks
Makes you aware, without an understanding of what it is that
You're doing. The hairstyle is nothing more than
A superficial lesson

Looks scratch the surface.
Fads scratch the surface.

It's about having an understanding
We need to have an understanding
Of our history,
The good and the bad parts,

So that we can fill in the blank parts within ourselves
We need to preserve our history;
Pass down our history
To prevent it from becoming a SUPERFICIAL LESSON

LET THAT STUFF GO

We have been conditioned by colonialism and slavery,
To believe that our beauty isn't good enough

We need to let that stuff go.

We have been conditioned by colonialism and slavery,
To believe our hair isn't good enough

We need to let that stuff go.

In some ways we are still suffering from the symptoms.

We need to let that stuff go.

Let that conditioning go!
Let that programming go!
Let that mindset go!

Let it go!

BACKSLIDING

We need to stop backsliding
And start accepting who we are

Our civil rights are valid; we fought for them
And won during the 1960s

Our beauty is valid; we protested for it
And it was accepted in the 1970s

The result was "Black is Beautiful" and the Afro

OUR BEAUTY IS VALID

Filed lawsuits for it by the thousands
In the 1980s so that braids could be accepted
In the workplace
We won the lawsuits

The result was being taken seriously
The way we are culturally

After the progress was made

We started sliding back

We need to stop backsliding
After progress
After every fight
And after every movement

We need to stand by our achievement
We need to stand by our struggle
And after we're through
Follow it through

BLACK HAIR ABSTRACT—WOMEN

Press-n-curl

Natural Hair

Press-n-curl

Wigs

Press-n-curl

Bouffant

Press-n-curl

Natural Hair

Press-n-curl

Afro

Relaxer

Braids

Relaxer

Jheri Curl

Relaxer

Weave

Relaxer

Locks

Relaxer

Twists

Relaxer

Natural Hair

Relaxer

BLACK HAIR ABSTRACT—MEN

Natural Hair

Conk

Natural Hair

Press-n-curl

Natural Hair

Afro

Natural Hair

Texturizer

Natural Hair

Shag Cut

Natural Hair

Jheri Curl

Natural Hair

S-Curl

Natural Hair

High Top Fade

Natural Hair

Locks

Natural Hair

Braids

Natural Hair

Twists

Natural Hair

AFROS TO…

Afros to natural hair
Afros to braids
Afros to relaxers
Afros to…

We now have variety when
It comes to how we style our hair.

Afros to locks
Afros to twists
Afros to cornrows
Afros to…

With all of the choices of hairstyles
That we now have, let's not lose sight
Of who we are.

Afros to blondes
Afros to wigs
Afros to weaves
Afros to…

GETTING TO THE ROOT OF THE MATTER

I am going to get right to it
Digging for the origin of the problem

Getting to the root of the matter

The negative feeling towards black hair
That some black people still harbor
Trying to find an answer

Getting to the root of the matter

The apprehension behind black hair
How did it come about?
Where did it start?

Getting to the root of the matter

Searching for more than just half the story
Working on getting the full story
Acknowledging that the problem does exist

Opening up the door for some soul searching
Opening up the door for some healing
Opening up the door for some much needed
DIALOGUE

Trying to find a solution
Searching for the origin

GETTING TO THE ROOT OF THE MATTER

OUR WAY OF BEING
Closing Poem

OUR WAY OF BEING

Our way of being is beautiful
Why do we feel that we have to compromise?

Our way of knowing is wonderful
Why do we feel that we have to change it?
Re-arrange it
To fit what others want
To fit what we assume others need?

Our way is uniquely ours and
Nobody else's and it's just fine
While most of us whine and complain
About who we are, how we are

Life is too precious for that type of thought.
Life is too precious to be wasted on
Petty concerns

Our way of walking is just fine
Our way of talking is just fine
Having curly hair is just fine
Having twisted hair is just fine
Having locked hair is just fine
Having braided hair is just fine
Having straight hair with cultural
Identity and appreciation
Is just fine

Being who we are, how we are
In our original form
The way that God
Created us to be
Should be just fine

It's time to stop suppressing
And start addressing
Our way of being
It's time to start
Without compromise
It's time

Bibliography

Note: Poetry is a creative endeavor, and the books that I have listed are just a few of the many books that I have read over the years that inspired me to write.

Akbar, Naim. Chains and Images of Psychological Slavery. New Mind Productions, 1984.

Angelou, Maya. I Know why the Caged Bird Sings. Bantam Books, 1967.

Banks, Ingrid. Hair Matters: Beauty, Power and Black Women's Consciousness New York UP 2000.

Bird, Ayana and Thorp, Lori. Hair Story: Untangling the Roots of Black Hair in America. Mac Millan Publishing Company, 2002.

Diop, Cheikh Anta. The African Origins of Civilization: Myth or Reality. Lawrence Hill & Co, 1989.

Dubois, W.E.B. The Souls of Black Folk. Dover Publications, 1994.

Fanon, Frantz. Black Skins, White Mask. New York: Grove/Atlantic Press, 1994.

Fanon, Frantz. The Wrenched of the Earth. New York: Grove/Atlantic Press, 1994.

Giddings, P. When and Where I Enter: The Impact of Black Women on Race and Sex In America. New York: William Morrow and Company, 1984.

Giovanni, Nikki. The Selected Poems of Nikki Giovanni. New York: William Morrow Company, 1996.

Hooks, Bell. Ain't I a Woman: Black Women and Feminism. Boston: South End Press, 1991.

Hughes, Langston. The Collected Poems of Langston Hughes. New York: Vintage Classic, 1995.

Jewell, Sue. From Mammy to Miss America and Beyond: Cultural Images and the Shaping of US Social Policy. New York: Rutledge, 1993.

Morrison, Toni. The Bluest Eyes. New York: Group, 1994.

Morrison, Toni. Playing in the Dark: Whiteness and the Literary Imagination. Cambridge: Harvard UP, 1992.

Rogers, J.A. From Superman to Man. Helga Rogers, 1990.

Rogers, J.A. Sex and Race Volumes I, II, III. Helga, Rogers, 1990.

Sharp, Sandra. Black Woman for Beginners. Writer Readers Publishing, 1993.

Welsing, Frances, Cress. The Isis Papers: The Keys To The Colors. Chicago: Third World Press, 1990.

West, Cornel. Race Matters. Knopf Publishing Group, 1994.

Williams, Chancellor. The Destruction of the Black Civilization. Chicago: Third World Press, 1992.

PHOTO PARTICIPANTS WITH BUSINESSES

THE LAST LYRICISTS—AZZIRAH & DIVINE .....MYSPACE.COM/THE LAST LYRICISTS

Patricia McNeal—JEWELRY DESIGNS.............PatriciaMcnll@yahoo.com

R.J. Rahman..www.RJRahman-Books.com

Nathaniel Borrell Dyer ....www.natbotheedge.com
A website that has fine arts
graphics and more ...

Earrings ....www.GottaHave-Earrings.com
Handmade Gemstone Earrings